Sandy Creek
122 Fifth Avenue
New York, NY 10011

ISBN-13: 978-1-4351-2354-0

Printed and bound in China

1 3 5 7 9 10 8 6 4 2

ROBIN hOOD

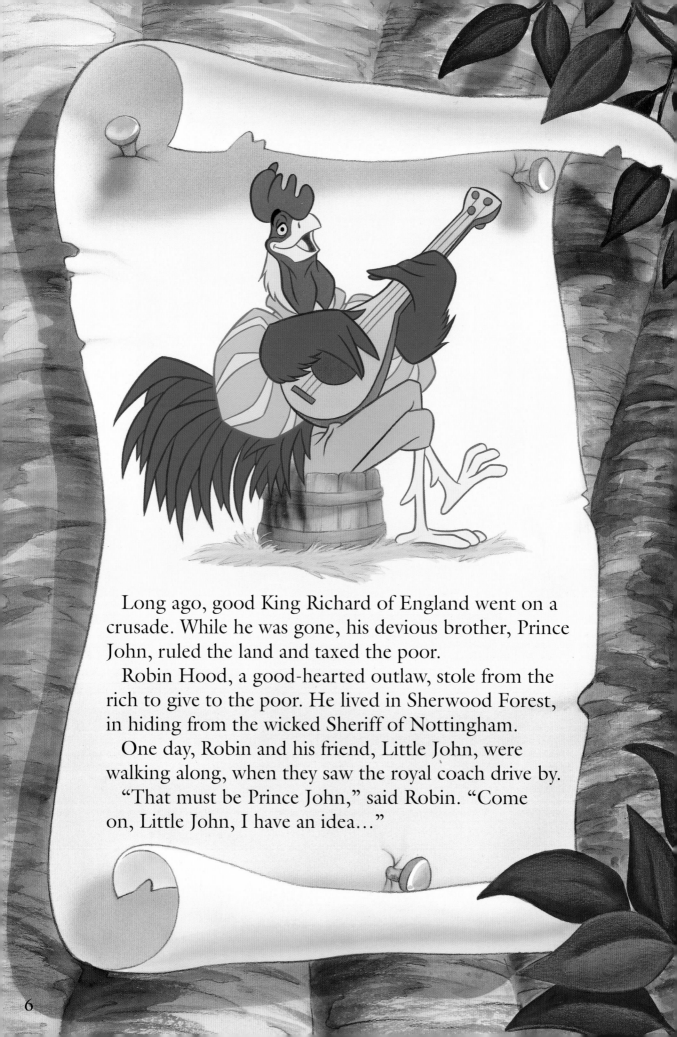

Long ago, good King Richard of England went on a crusade. While he was gone, his devious brother, Prince John, ruled the land and taxed the poor.

Robin Hood, a good-hearted outlaw, stole from the rich to give to the poor. He lived in Sherwood Forest, in hiding from the wicked Sheriff of Nottingham.

One day, Robin and his friend, Little John, were walking along, when they saw the royal coach drive by.

"That must be Prince John," said Robin. "Come on, Little John, I have an idea…"

Inside the royal coach, Prince John, and his loyal adviser, Sir Hiss, the snake, were counting the gold he had got from taxing the people of England.

"Sire, I have always admired how you manage to take from the poor and give to the rich," lisped Sir Hiss.

They both laughed as the money trickled through Prince John's fingers.

Meanwhile, Robin Hood and Little John were lying in wait.
They were determined not to let the prince escape with all the taxes.
   The two outlaws were masters of disguise and they had hatched a
clever plan. Dressed as gypsies, they waited by the side of the road
for the royal coach to pass by.
   Robin cried, "Do you need a fortune teller?"
   "We can bring you great wealth and happiness!" said Little John.
   Prince John could not resist. He told the guards to stop the coach.

Sir Hiss tried to warn the prince that the two gypsies could be bandits.

"What nonsense!" said Prince John. "There's no such thing as female bandits!"

He allowed the two fortune tellers to kiss his hands in greeting—and Little John sucked the jewels from his royal rings with his mouth! Prince John didn't notice a thing and invited them inside the coach to tell his fortune.

While Robin was telling the gullible prince's fortune, Little John busied himself with the gold. He slipped underneath the chest and drilled a hole in the bottom with his dagger.

He caught the falling coins in his shirt—without the royal rhino guards noticing a thing!

Robin and Little John stole broaches, bags of gold and even the golden hubcaps from the coach. They were so laden with treasures they could hardly carry everything. They planned to return it to the poor people of Nottingham.

By the time Prince John realized that he had been tricked, it was already too late. Furiously he called to his soldiers, "After them, you idiots!"

But even in their long skirts, Robin and Little John were too fast for the guards and escaped with their loot.

Prince John was beside himself with rage. He had posters hung up across the country offering a reward for the capture of Robin Hood.

He also ordered the Sheriff of Nottingham to collect more taxes to make up for the stolen gold.

The evil sheriff loved nothing better than collecting taxes from the poor. During his tour around the city, he hummed happily to himself.

One day, the sheriff noticed Friar Tuck hurrying along the road. The sheriff knew that the kind-hearted friar would try to help the poor.

He followed the friar to see what he was up to. Friar Tuck went to the blacksmith's forge and handed him a bag full of gold coins.

"Pssst, Otto, here's some money from Robin Hood," he whispered.

But the cunning sheriff was listening at the door. When he burst in, Friar Tuck quickly hid the gold in Otto's bandaged leg.

"Oh, please have pity on me, Sheriff," begged Otto. "As you can see, I have a broken leg and I have fallen behind with my work."

"But you have also fallen behind with your taxes," replied the sheriff.

"Have you no heart, Sheriff!" cried Friar Tuck. "Can't you see he is suffering? Come, sit here and rest, Otto."

As Otto sat down, the coins in his bandage jangled. The sheriff grabbed his leg and roughly shook the coins out into his hand.

But that was only the beginning of his day as the royal tax collector. Next, the sheriff visited poor Mother Rabbit and her children. It was Skippy's birthday, and the whole family had saved up to give him a single gold coin.

As soon as the lad had unwrapped his present, the sheriff forced him to hand it over.

As poor Skippy wept, there was a knock at the door. A blind beggar was asking for money. Mother Rabbit took pity on the beggar and offered him a chair by the fire.

The beggar sat down. "Tell me," he said, "is it somebody's birthday here today?"

"Yes, sir," sobbed Skippy. "But the evil sheriff, stole my birthday present."

Suddenly the beggar whipped off his disguise—it was Robin Hood! Robin gave Skippy a bow and arrow and his very own hat. Then he gave Mother Rabbit a bag full of coins.

"Bless you, Robin Hood!" cried Mother Rabbit.

Skippy couldn't wait to try out his new gift. So he went outside with his sisters and his friend Toby, the tortoise.

Skippy's eldest sister, Sis, warned her brother not to aim too high, but Skippy was far too excited to listen to her.

"I know what I'm doing. Watch this!" he cried.

Skippy released the bow. The arrow flew high into the air and soared straight over the castle wall!

Skippy slipped through a small gate in the courtyard to go and look for his arrow.

Inside, he met Maid Marian and Lady Kluck, her lady-in-waiting. Maid Marion spotted the other children and invited them inside. The little girls wanted to know whether she and Robin Hood were sweethearts.

Marian showed them where Robin had once carved their initials into a tree. She hoped that he had not forgotten her and dreamed of the day when they would be married.

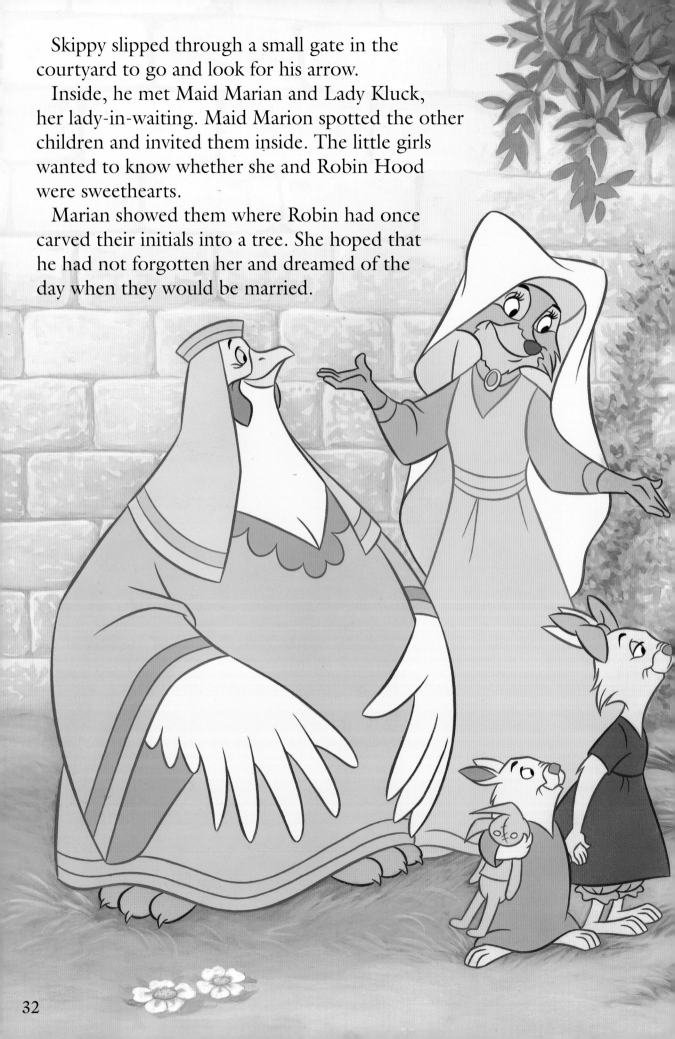

Little did Maid Marian know, but back in Sherwood Forest, Robin was thinking about the very same thing.

Just then Friar Tuck arrived to tell Robin about the Tournament of Golden Arrows that would be held in Nottingham the very next day!

"Somehow, I don't think we'll be invited!" laughed Robin.

However, when Friar Tuck told him that Maid Marian would kiss the winner, Robin immediately hatched a plan to compete in the tournament!

The day of the archery tournament had arrived, and Prince John was very pleased with himself. He planned to use Maid Marian as bait to lure Robin Hood out of hiding.

Sir Hiss bowed to the prince and congratulated him on his brilliant idea.

"Your plan to capture Robin Hood is ingenious, Sire."

Robin Hood and Little John arrived at the tournament in disguise. They couldn't resist the opportunity to poke fun at the prince.

Little John introduced himself as Sir Reginald, Duke of Chutney. "Ah, my Lord, my highly esteemed king and ruler, I bow before you!" he said.

The flattered prince didn't suspect a thing and invited Sir Reginald to join him in the royal box.

Meanwhile, disguised as a stork, Robin filed past the royal box along with the other contestants.

He stopped before Maid Marian and handed her a flower.

"Sweet maid," he said, "forgive me, but it is an honor to meet such a charming lady. Hopefully I will win your kiss."

As soon as their eyes met, Maid Marian knew that the stork was her beloved Robin Hood.

By the end of the tournament, only Robin and the Sheriff of Nottingham were left in the competition. The sheriff was taking no chances. He was going to win, even if he had to cheat!

When it was Robin's turn, the Sheriff tipped his bow from behind. Robin's shot went in completely the wrong direction. Robin quickly fired another shot, which knocked the first arrow back on course. His arrow whistled through the air, then hit the target with a perfect bull's-eye! Robin had won!

Robin was led to the royal box to receive his prize. But Prince John knew there was only one man who was capable of such a shot.

He pretended to congratulate Robin. "Our most cordial royal congratulations. I pronounce you the winner, or should I say—the loser!"

With these words he tore off Robin's disguise and ordered his guards to arrest Robin.

"I hereby condemn you to . . . death," growled the prince.

Robin's friends thought all hope was lost. So, imagine their astonishment when Prince John suddenly changed his mind, and commanded his men to release Robin!

Little John had been hiding behind the prince all along. He pushed a dagger into his back and told him what to say.

Robin was released, but before he and his friends could escape, the prince alerted the guards to attack.

In the middle of a wild chase, Robin rescued Maid Marian and asked for her hand in marriage.

"Oh, Robin, I thought you would never ask!" she replied.

Little John, Robin, and even Lady Kluck fought bravely against the guards, and finally, they all escaped to the safety of Sherwood Forest.

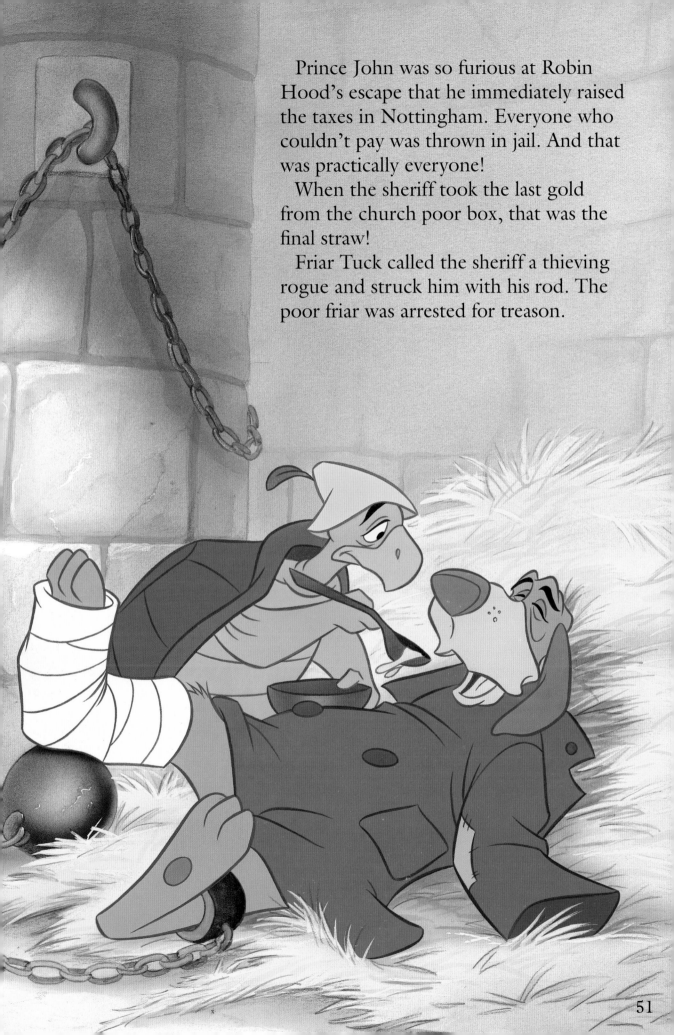

Prince John was so furious at Robin Hood's escape that he immediately raised the taxes in Nottingham. Everyone who couldn't pay was thrown in jail. And that was practically everyone!

When the sheriff took the last gold from the church poor box, that was the final straw!

Friar Tuck called the sheriff a thieving rogue and struck him with his rod. The poor friar was arrested for treason.

Prince John spotted a marvelous opportunity to trap Robin Hood again. He ordered Friar Tuck to be sentenced to death, knowing that Robin would try to save his friend.

Sir Hiss was not completely convinced by the idea.

"But, Sire," he objected. "Hang Friar Tuck? A man of the church?"

"Yes, you sniveling snake," replied Prince John. "And when our valiant hero tries to free the friar my guards will be there. Ha, ha, ha!"

Prince John was right. The night before Friar Tuck's execution, Robin crept back into the castle. Disguised as a night-watchman, he stole the keys from the sheriff's belt while he was sleeping and gave them to Little John.

"You free brother Tuck and the others, I'm going to visit the royal treasury," he said.

Robin wasn't going to leave without taking the taxes that belonged to the people.

Little John helped everyone escape—
Mother Rabbit and her children, Otto the
blacksmith, and Friar Tuck. They planned
to meet Robin outside the castle walls, and
help him steal back the gold.

"Come on everyone!" whispered Little
John, as he led the way.

Meanwhile, Robin crept into the royal bedchamber where the prince and Sir Hiss were sleeping peacefully among the bags of gold.

Rigging up a rope and pully to lower the gold down to his friends, Robin began to slip all the tax money out of the castle.

"Quick!" Robin cried to his men down below. "Grab the gold and run for the forest!"

Robin attached the last bag of gold to the rope, and was about to make his escape when Sir Hiss suddenly woke up! He tried to stop Robin by grabbing onto one of the bags with his teeth. He wrapped his tail around Prince John's leg and so all three were pulled out of the window!

"Guards, guards! My gold! He's escaping with my gold!" cried Prince John, as he floated high above the castle.

The guards sprang into action and the night sky was peppered with arrows.

Robin dropped safely to the ground and ran to join Friar Tuck and the others. They jumped on a cart along with the bags of gold and ran across the drawbridge. But when Robin went back to rescue one of Mother Rabbit's children, he was trapped inside the castle.

"Run," he shouted. "Don't worry about me!"

Little John pulled the cart into the safety of the forest and Robin was left to fend for himself.

By now the castle was swarming with angry guards and it was all Robin could do to dodge their arrows, spears and swords.

The sheriff chased Robin up into a tower. He tried to attack Robin with a burning torch, and accidently set the curtains on fire. Before long, the whole tower was in flames. Robin fled to the roof and jumped into the moat just in time.

On the other side of the moat Little John and Skippy were waiting in the hope that they might spot Robin in the water. Just as they were about to give up hope, up popped their hero—tired and wet—but alive!

Thanks to Robin and his men, the kingdom was safe for King Richard's return. When the king saw his castle in ruins and learnt how his greedy brother had treated his people, he was very angry.

He threw Prince John, Sir Hiss, and the Sheriff of Nottingham in prison, and sentenced them to work in a quarry.

King Richard pardoned Robin Hood. Now that he was no longer an outlaw, nothing stood in the way of his marriage to Maid Marian. The happy couple invited all their friends from Nottingham to celebrate their wedding.

As Robin and Marian left the church, everyone cried, "Long live Robin Hood! Long live King Richard!"

Peace and joy reigned in Nottingham once again.